For Tom, Eleanor, John and Rachel
P. B.

For my beloved daughter Sorcha
and Sylvester, her cat
G. S.

PUFFIN/VIKING

Published by the Penguin Group
Penguin Books Ltd, 27 Wrights Lane, London W8 5TZ, England
Penguin Putnam Inc., 375 Hudson Street, New York, New York 10014, USA
Penguin Books Australia Ltd, Ringwood, Victoria, Australia
Penguin Books Canada Ltd, 10 Alcorn Avenue, Toronto, Ontario, Canada M4V 3B2
Penguin Books (NZ) Ltd, Private Bag 102902, NSMC, Auckland, New Zealand

Penguin Books Ltd, Registered Offices: Harmondsworth, Middlesex, England

First published by Viking 1998
1 3 5 7 9 10 8 6 4 2

Published in Puffin Books 1999
3 5 7 9 10 8 6 4 2

Text copyright © Philippa Butler, 1998
Illustrations copyright © George Smith, 1998
All rights reserved.

The moral right of the author and illustrator has been asserted

Made and printed in Italy by Printer Trento Srl

Except in the United States of America, this book is sold subject to the condition that it shall not,
by way of trade or otherwise, be lent, re-sold, hired out, or otherwise circulated without the publisher's prior consent
in any form of binding or cover other than that in which it is published and without a similar condition
including this condition being imposed on the subsequent purchaser

British Library Cataloguing in Publication Data
A CIP catalogue record for this book is available from the British Library

ISBN 0–670–87177–X Hardback
ISBN 0–140–56240–0 Paperback

PAWPRINTS in TIME

Philippa Butler

Illustrated by George Smith

PUFFIN

VIKING

No one knew Cat's real name or where he came from. He just arrived one winter's evening and miaowed outside Anna's window until she let him in. And then he stayed.

Cat was old – older than anyone could know. But his black fur was still rich and soft, and his green eyes still glowed like emeralds.

I am a cat with stories to tell.

Throughout the winter Cat slept by the fire. In the summer he slept in the sun. But every night, summer and winter, he disappeared, returning only after everyone was asleep, and miaowing outside Anna's window until she let him in.

I am a cat with stories to tell.

Then Anna would make a space for him on the bed and Cat would curl up beside her as she drifted back into sleep.

I am a cat with stories to tell.

I
will tell
you stories of
ancient Egypt,
where cats were
gods. Now they lie
buried beneath the
pyramids with
the Pharaohs,
still wearing their
gold and jewels,
curled up to sleep
for thousands
of years.

I
will tell
you stories of
ancient Rome
and the cats
and the children
who played
together on
cool mosaic
floors.

◇⊠⊠⊠◇

I

will tell
you stories
of the long silk
road from China
and the cats who
waited for the
merchants
to return.

I

will tell
you stories
of the mountain
temples of Tibet
and the cats who
worshipped there.
Wherever a cat
goes, people still
say he brings
good luck
with him.

I

will tell
you stories
of the cats
who watched
the rise of
the great
cathedrals...

. . . **A**nd
chased along the
corridors of court.
Painted, chiselled,
carved and
drawn, still they
purr silently.

I

will tell you
stories of great
sea voyages.
How cats
travelled across
the world hunting
rats and mice in
the tall sailing ships.
How they know
the things sailors
never know.

How
they have
seen old
and new
worlds.

How
they have
been stroked
by different
hands and
have sat by
different fires.

No one ever took any notice of Cat but Anna. No one else stroked his fur. Or opened the door for him. Or gave him saucers of cream. Or moved his cushion closer to the fire. But if anyone said, 'Now that's a cat who's had nine lives!' Anna would just smile and remember how she had seen lives they could never see and had shared the stories only a cat could tell.